The Dreamer Entrepreneur ...

Let me introduce you to a
little eleven-year-old girl named
Isabella, who everyone calls,
Izzy. Why does she need an
introduction? Well, she is an
amazing eleven-year-old who was
born as an entrepreneur. At the
age of eight, she started making
bracelets for herself. She was happy
with her beautiful bracelets.

She asked her mom if she could make them for others and sell them around the neighborhood. Her mom agreed it was a good idea for Izzy. She sold bracelet after bracelet and people loved them.

Izzy would sit in her room every afternoon hard at work making bracelets to sell around the neighborhood. Every day Izzy thought about how she could sell more bracelets. One afternoon Izzy and her mom were baking cookies as they did so many times, it was their favorite thing to do together. Izzy thought to herself, wow I wonder if I baked cookies would anyone buy them.

So, Izzy with a big smile, said Mom do you think I could bake cookies and sell them around our local neighborhood? Her mom said, well I believe you could get some people to buy them remember everyone does not like cookies.

Izzy with determination in her eyes, was overjoyed with a brand-new business adventure. She started baking cookies and selling them to her friends and the local neighborhoods. Her friends and neighborhood loved them and asked when she could make more cookies and bracelets.

The summertime was ending, and Izzy soon would have to close shop and focus on school. Izzy was happy and sad, happy because she loved going to school and unhappy because she loved making bracelets and cookies for everyone.

For an eleven-year-old, Izzy was quite fascinated with business. She went and asked her mom and dad, what they thought it took to be successful in business. They said, well Izzy it takes knowledge, resources, money, lots of time, and people to help you.

Izzy thought to herself I know I can do this; I can do business! Izzy was so determined that this was what she wanted to do. She thought, I can save my allowance every week and when next summer comes around, I will be ready. Dad always says you are nothing without a good plan.

After some time had passed, one of the most amazing things happened to Izzy, she had a dream that would change her life forever. She dreamed about business. She saw herself at a huge event in her city, where she was selling bracelets and cookies. People were lining up to buy them. All her friends were there helping her get them all sold. Izzy woke up with such joy. She rushed downstairs to tell her mom all about her dream.

Izzy said Mom last night I had a dream, and, in my dream, I saw myself at some huge event right here in our city selling bracelets and cookies. So many people were lined up to buy them. Mom, I saw all my friends there helping me. Her mom said Izzy that was quite the dream you had last night.

My dear Izzy, I know you have enjoyed making bracelets and cookies for our neighborhoods, but to run a successful business takes a lot of money, money you do not have. Izzy says, Mom, you always tell me that if you spend everything, you will never be able to buy what you need or want. So, I have been saving my allowance for months now. I have not spent any money.

Please, Mom, Izzy says with desperation on her face. Her mom says, Izzy, you mean to tell me all this time you have been saving your allowance and working extra hard around the house so that you could start a business? Exactly, Mom. I want to do this, Mom. I need to talk to your father about this her mom said.

The next day, Izzy would get the most exciting news of her life. Her mom said yes! Izzy's mom said, Izzy because you want to do this so much and you have been saving all your money, we will allow you to do this and help you. It must be all hands, on deck!

Izzy's bedroom also became her office, in the afternoons she would make bracelet after bracelet and even invite her friends to help her. She was preparing for her big day. With the summertime now upon them, the new things to do at home were making bracelets and cookies.

The big day was finally here. She sat up her stan at the local city stadium. She looked around and saw her friends right there. It was just like her dream.

People lined up at her stan to buy her bracelets and cookies. With a smile of sheer confidence, Izzy was thrilled that she was selling out of all her bracelets and cookies. Her dream had come true!

Tears began to roll down her face
and she thanked her friends for
helping her.

One of her customers asked her:
Little girl what do you want
to be when you grow up? With
big confidence, she said: Be an
entrepreneur!

Izzy was tied and happy all at the same time. Soon her friends were asking her to help them start their businesses. She was known as the "little dreamer entrepreneur". She had proven at eleven that determination will help you achieve your dreams.

The End.